Let's Talk About Pagan Festivals

Let's Talk About Pagan Festivals

Siusaidh Ceanadach

MOON
BOOKS

Winchester, UK
Washington, USA

First published by Moon Books, 2012
Moon Books is an imprint of John Hunt Publishing Ltd., Laurel House, Station Approach,
Alresford, Hants, SO24 9JH, UK
office1@jhpbooks.net
www.johnhuntpublishing.com
www.moon-books.net

For distributor details and how to order please visit the 'Ordering' section on our website.

Text copyright: Siusaidh Ceanadach 2012

ISBN: 978 1 78099 463 5

A CIP catalogue record for this book is available from the British Library.

Design: Stuart Davies

Printed and bound by CPI Group (UK) Ltd, Croydon, CR0 4YY

We operate a distinctive and ethical publishing philosophy in all
areas of our business, from our global network of authors to
production and worldwide distribution.

CONTENTS

Acknowledgements

I would like to thank the Acredyke Nursery School, Robroyston, Glasgow, for asking me to write a little booklet about Imbolc that led to a request for more festivals and in turn resulted in this book.

I would also like to acknowledge the help and support that our clan cousin Maria Moloney has given me, her continued friendship, knowledge and patience seems to be unending. The quiet stable support of Trevor Greenfield is also greatly appreciated.

I must also mention my own grandchildren, all seven of them for without their presence in my life I would never have been prompted to write for children.

I should also like to thank *Nina Falaise, the gifted visionary artist who has produced the cover for this book and all the drawings.

Nina Falaise was born in Skipton, Yorkshire.
Nina has been an active participant in the Western Mystery Tradition for many years, contributing her experience of dance, mask making and choreography to ceremonial rituals. Nina is a visionary artist, who's art is inspired through ritual, meditation and her ongoing studies of the Great Work. Nina has illustrated for several books, including, A Ceremony for Every Occasion by Siusaidh Ceanadach, Daughters of Danu by Piet Ceanadach and What Brave Bulls Do by Rohase Piercy. For artwork commissions by Nina, contact: nina.falaise@yahoo.com

Introduction

There are eight major festivals, and each is roughly six weeks apart. These follow the year's turning and are tuned into nature and the seasons. Some of the festivals are well known, Beltane and Samhain (Halloween) are two of them and they are at opposite times of the year. In fact there are four solar festivals, two solstices and two equinoxes, these mark the path of the Sun (it's actually the Earth that moves and not the Sun, for this is an illusion and it's easier to think of the Sun growing and getting warmer and then colder).

There are also four "cross festivals" these were fire celebrations and folk would build a big bonfire, light candles and have a celebration. The four cross festivals are: Imbolc (February 2nd), Beltane (May 1st), Lughnasadh (August 1st) and Samhain (October 31st).

Put together they divide the year into eight festivals referred to as "The Wheel of the Year". Each of them is connected to nature and its changing seasons, to what's going in the farmer's year and to special things to remember through the year.

Imbolc is the first Pagan festival of the Wheel of the Year after Midwinter. The Pagan Celtic Year ends at Samhain, but for the purpose of this book and for little children I think it may be easier for them to link early spring to new starts and so I am starting with Imbolc.

Imbolc – "First Milk"

Teachers, Parents and Guardians Notes

Imbolc was dedicated to Brigit to welcome in the start of the spring.

At Midwinter, we celebrated the birth of the Divine Child, the light of inspiration and hope. We teach that the Mother Goddess labours all through the longest night to give birth to the new child, the tiny Sun. This is a myth, a story we tell our children and young ones to help them understand. Naturally, you and I know that it is the orbit of the Earth around our star, the Sun, which causes the change in the seasons, and we know the Sun will get stronger after Midwinter. But it's not just the basic facts we are talking about here, in order to encourage a faith, we need to put our thoughts into story form for the sake of our young ones. Then it is a good idea to teach in story form. It's difficult for little ones to understand the ever-changing seasons, the farmer's year, the birth, growth and then death of our animals.

We are told by our own elders that Brigit was very fond of animals. Saint Bridget as she became to the Christian Church was said to have a healing mission especially for animals and it is said that she helped cure many a sick animal.

February 2nd is the day in which we celebrate the Goddess Brigit. We connect to her in three ways and indeed some stories tell of her having two sisters of the same age. She is a Goddess of the Hearth, Goddess of Smithcraft and Poetry, and she is also the healing Goddess of Birth, and Lactation. Christian myths tell of her being the midwife of the Baby Jesus and she certainly does link with midwives.

In early times, the hearth was a very important part of family life, not only did it provide a place where food was cooked, it was the heat source of the home and it was around the hearth that the family and friends would sit in the evening and sing songs, play music and tell stories.

A blacksmith was also a very important man in a village for without him the horses would not have suitable shoes to enable them to do the heavy work needed on a farm, and the blacksmith would also make and mend farm tools as well as knives, swords and spears — all the things needed to kill and butcher meat for the family.

In Ireland and amongst other Celtic tribes, Brigit is Mary of the Gaels, the main Goddess called upon and called to for many different reasons throughout the year. Myth tells us that the first Brigit was the daughter of the Dagda, the good God and one of the Tuatha Dé Danann, the children of Danu, that she was the half-sister of Cermait, Aengus, Midir and Bodb Derg. She is a classic triple Goddess.

Brigit gathered herself a group of young women whom she taught the skills required for healing, astronomy, herbcraft and healing. These priestesses became important people within their villages and tribes; they were the midwives, the healers and they taught others how to work with the changing seasons. At some stage back beyond recorded time, following a great war, Brigit and other Dananns chose to take to the land beneath the ground. She travelled on, leaving a high or chief priestess in charge of the group of women who kept a flame burning night and day all year round bar one and continued to teach all the skills needed in their roles in early tribal life.

I am sure you know the story that eventually Christianity came to these lands and Pagan ways were swallowed up into a new faith, but Brigit was so very important to the Gaels that the Church made her a Saint.

So in honour of her very important role in our lives we remember her special feast day, we remember her role of healer, especially of birth and lactation. This is why we link this festival to first milk, the liquid produced by a mother for her young to give them antibodies that are needed in order to help fight disease. We link this time to the mother sheep, the ewes who are getting ready to lamb and she is also linked to most white flowers but especially snowdrops.

Gemstones linked to this time of year would be Moonstone and also Bloodstone according to astrological sources. I would personally pick white or milky white gemstones, any stone that brings to mind milk or snowdrops. When picking crystals and gemstones each person must follow their own instinct and when you come to dedicate your stone keep the reason clearly in your mind the whole time because like all magical matters it's the intent that is the most important.

Imbolc (Im-olk) is a festival of light to welcome the spring and say goodbye to the winter.

In the fields the ewes, the mother sheep, were getting bigger; their tummies were getting big because they were growing tiny baby lambs inside them. Soon it would be time for the baby lambs to be born.

The Ewe's udders, the place where the baby lambs would suck their milk from were filling up with a very special "first milk" (this is what the word Imbolc means).

The snowdrops were popping their heads out of the cool earth, and the ground was getting ever so slightly warmer.

A Story for Imbolc

Lucy lived on a farm up in the hills, her dad kept a large flock of sheep and her mummy was always busy cooking, soon she would be feeding the tiniest lambs that could not feed from their own mothers. Sometimes the ewes had three lambs and were not able to feed all three, so the smallest were brought up to the kitchen in Lucy's house and fed with a bottle of milk, they had a little warm box to sleep in.

Lucy woke up one morning and quickly got ready to go out with her dad to look at the sheep. She had favourites and one of them looked very fat yesterday and was behaving oddly. She kept wiggling backwards, and went round and round in the same patch of ground. "She's ready to lamb that one!" said Dad.

Lucy looked worriedly at the ewe.

"Don't you worry, she'll be fine lass," said Dad. "And if she has more than two you can have the other one." He laughed. (Because he never ever thought she would have more than one lamb)

So out they went into the field, with Lucy sitting behind her dad on the quad bike, both wearing a safety helmet. As they worked their way around the field, her dad picked up the new little lambs and sprayed some brown stuff called iodine on their tummies. This was to make sure the stump of the cord that had linked the lambs to their mothers while they were growing inside their tummies didn't become infected. He sprayed a number on the mother sheep and the same number on the baby lamb. He also gave them a squirt of something from a bottle that the vet had suggested was a very good idea.

At last they came to Lucy's favourite ewe and my goodness gracious me! How many lambs do you think she had? One? No, Two? No, she had three little lambs!

Lucy's dad was very surprised and he got to work spraying their tummies with a quick spray of the iodine and also gave them a squirt of the stuff from a bottle that the vet had sent. He was just spraying numbers on their backs when he looked up at Lucy and said, "This little one is not going to get enough to drink, her mum has only two teats, she can't feed three." And he looked very sad for a moment and then looked up at Lucy. "If you are prepared to work hard and feed this little lamb every two hours to start with, then if you can raise her properly, she's yours!"

Lucy said she would love to try to raise the lamb and they took the little one back up to the farmhouse.

Mum found a cardboard box and they put some straw in it.

"That will have to do for now," said Mum. "But in a couple of days she will be moved out into the lambing sheds and you are going to have to go and feed her and look after her for several weeks."

"I can do it, I can do it," said Lucy, and her chest filled up and she looked all of a sudden more like an older child and less like a little one.

So Lucy fed and raised that little lamb, and she grew up to be a very beautiful, but tame ewe. She was let out with the flock in the summer but she still came up to Lucy when she went to see her and called her name.

What do you think she called her baby lamb?

She called her Brigit after the Goddess Brigit and because she was born so very close to Imbolc.

End of story.

More About Imbolc

At this time of the year, the family, and many of the people all over the countryside would ask a blessing on all the new born, and on all the "first milk". Candles were white, the colour of milk and any biscuits and cakes would be white with white icing on top.

Any decorations, if they had some would be white as well, the colour of milk.

The special person, the special Goddess that people talked to and said prayers to at this time of the year was "Brigit", she was said to have come from Ireland and looked after animals, helped people with poetry and helped the blacksmith as well. She had three main roles to play.

To ask for her blessing people would simply close their eyes and talk to "Brigit", this kind of thing is often called a "prayer".

The family would make a little bed and put little pieces of cloth into it, they would then leave it indoors by the hearth fire, or in a warm place and say something like this:

"Brigit, Brigit, your bed is ready, come out of the cold and sleep in this nice warm bed."

Sometimes the grown-ups would make a little straw doll and carefully dress it and in the morning they would put the new "Brigit doll" into her new bed.

Once Brigit was welcomed into the house and into their lives, they would know that she would bless them all and help look after all the newborn lambs.

Nice Things to Do for Imbolc

1   Using an old cardboard box get a grown-up to help you cut it open to make a bed. Paint it white and put some cloth material in the bed.
2   Dress a little doll in something white, or make a doll picture and get a grown-up to cut in out and put it into your bed.
3   You can say … *Here's your new bed Brigit, come and sleep in it!*
4   Get a grown-up to help you cut up some white crêpe paper into wide strips, attach one end of the paper around your wrist and run around the room, waving your arms and letting all the strips make waves. Blow the clouds away and welcome the spring … *Go away clouds, welcome spring!*
5   Be a lamb, crawl around the room and make the noise a new lamb would make, *baa, baa* and with luck the little lambs will hear your voice and know it's time to be born and play in the fields with their mums.
6   Make little white biscuits and ice them with white icing.
7   Have a nice drink of milk and maybe a biscuit.

Basic Moon Biscuits for Festivals

You will need:

A plastic covered apron to keep your clothes clean

A crescent shaped cutter

A bowl to mix the dry ingredients in

A little bowl to mix the wet ingredients in

Kitchen scales to weigh the ingredients

A big metal spoon, a small teaspoon

A wooden spoon or, with a grown-up's help, a hand mixer

A sieve to sift the lumps out of the flour

Ingredients

250g butter, softened

140g caster sugar

1 egg yolk

2 tsp vanilla extract

300g plain flour

Method

First, wash your hands and then weigh all your ingredients out and have them ready for mixing.

1 Soften the butter and then add the sugar into the butter and mix until soft and creamy.

2 Beat the egg yolk and vanilla together and then add this into the butter and sugar.

3 Shake the flour through the sieve into the mixture and mix carefully with a metal spoon.

4 As the dough becomes sticky, remove the spoon and with your hands mix the dough into a ball.

5 Sprinkle some flour onto the table and put your ball of dough onto the table in the middle of the sprinkled flour.

6 Roll the mixture out until it's about 3 cm thick, or thicker if you want your biscuits more like cookies.

7 Cut crescent moon shapes out with your cutter. You can cut some round circles for a full moon shape as well.

8 Place the biscuits onto a greased baking tray and sprinkle a little bit of very fine caster sugar over them.

9 *Bake in a pre-heated oven at 180C or gas mark 4 for 15 minutes.

10 Take the cooked biscuits out of the oven and cool them on a wire rack.

*You must get a grown-up helper for this part because ovens are very hot!

Tip, if your grown-up helper does burn their fingers, hold their hand under a cold tap, turn on the water to cool the burn down quickly. It needs about half a minute to cool a burn down to stop a nasty blister coming up!

Some Little Prayers for Imbolc

Lovely Brigit, your snowdrops peep through the snow and show off their pretty petals, help us to see the beauty in your flowers, thank you for sending us such pretty flowers.

Mother Earth, we feel so small when we see photos of your wonderful planet. Help us to understand about your ever-changing seasons.

Father Sky, the Sun warms the Earth more and more each day, please warm my heart a little more each day too.

Spring Equinox

Teachers, Parents and Guardians Notes

As the Sun moves into Aries around the 21st or 22nd March, which starts a new year of journey through the Zodiac belt, here on Earth the day and the night become equal. Everything is in balance, the Earth is about to burst into action for the summer months, the hare is busy choosing a mate and countless boxing matches go on with males trying to get the attention of the females. If she's not quite ready to be mated, she will box even harder and run faster. At one stage, it was thought that it was the males who were boxing, but modern research has established that it is in fact the female who is boxing with the male.

The female hare scoops a dip into the ground and lines her nest with soft under-fur where she has her leverets. As soon as they leave their nest, ground nesting birds take over and lay their eggs into the old discarded nest. And it was this that first made people think that in some way the hares were producing eggs and they became linked to Ostara, the Anglo-Saxon Goddess of spring.

Ostara comes with the March winds and brings the spring into full abundance. She is associated with the hare, which became the "Easter Bunny" once Christianity had taken over Ostara and linked it into the "rise from the dead" of their God, and thus Easter came into being. The majority of the population accepted that they could still have their coloured eggs, their bright spring flowers, new hats and with just a small change in the spelling, Ostara became Easter.

But the Christian Easter is a feast that moves according to the Full Moon each year, it falls on the first Sunday after Passover and yet the Spring Equinox is always almost the same, March 21st or 22nd depending on the position of our orbit around the Sun.

So how do Pagans see this time of year? It's a time of great balance and of new beginnings; it heralds the start of the light half of the year and brings the trees, flowers and the crops into full growth. At both spring and autumn it is an opportunity to bring to mind all the things which have not been very good throughout the winter, both mentally, spiritually and physically. A chance to put these things down onto paper and burn them, to see them go up in flames, which leaves a fresh new start for the summer. (Naturally we do this out of doors and we have a little cast iron pot in which to contain these pieces of paper).

With the light increasing now, chickens that are kept in natural conditions will start to lay each day, some even start earlier. At first, they lay perhaps every three days as the light grows each day but by now they will be in full lay, giving us an abundance of eggs. So it's no problem at all to put some aside to dye and decorate.

In 2011, I noticed that chocolate "Easter" eggs were on sale in supermarkets soon after Christmas, and it seems that shops have jumped in here and our pretty painted hardboiled chicken's eggs have been taken over by mass produced chocolate eggs with perhaps about 400 percent profit on their sales. It really is high time to encourage children to go back to the natural eggs and the little competitions for the prettiest or the most colourful.

A Story for the Spring Equinox

Tansy had a little cousin, he was called Niall, and he had just passed his fourth winter, like Tansy he was not old enough to help or do any chores yet, but he wanted to learn.

The children had noticed that the days were getting longer but there was still a long night too. The birds had started to lay their eggs and some were picked up and eaten by the family. All around the village the flowers of springtime were starting to flower, very soon the old Druid said it would soon be equal day and equal night. What kind of a celebration were they going to have? They went off to see the old Druid to ask him all about it.

They found the Druid sitting crossed legged on the ground with a faraway look on his face, as if he was dreaming with his eyes open.

"Please sir," said Niall. "We have noticed that we have a longer daytime but still it seems as if the night is long."

"You have noticed have you?" said the Druid. "You are right and very soon we will have an equal day and an equal night."

"Are we going to have another day's holiday?" asked Niall.

"Yes we are, children," said the Druid. "We are going to celebrate the Spring Equinox."

The children went back to their homes in the village and watched over the next few days.

Niall's mother picked some herbs and some roots and made a dye and then put some of the eggs into the coloured water and cooked them. The eggs came out all pretty colours and were put in a bowl to share with all the others in the family.

They had fresh milk and some bread. Mead, which is a honey wine, was passed around the family and everyone took most of the day off work to celebrate.

In the fields, the hares who had been playing chase and boxing each other were quieter now and they had little baby hares called leverets. This season is all about spring, with bright green and yellow things.

There is a special person that some people who follow the old ways talk to at this time and her name is Ostara. Ostara is the Goddess of spring, she brings all the springtime things with her when she comes.

End of story.

Things to Do for the Spring Equinox

1 Hard boil some white eggs, then soak them in vegetable dye to make them a different colour, then you can take a wax crayon and draw a pattern on the egg and then soak it in a different colour. The wax will stop the second dye covering your pattern, you will need a grown-up to help you with all of this.

2 Make a spring hat by taking a paper plate, cut out the centre and stick ribbons on the edge to tie under your chin. Decorate the edge of the plate with flowers, shapes and ribbons.

3 Draw, colour and cut out pictures of yellow chicks and arrange them on a big piece of paper, then you can draw some eggs and broken shells to show where all the chicks came from.

4 The animal to try to copy this time would be a hare. They have very long legs and jump a lot so you need to crouch down as small as a hare and then jump up in the air, you can do this all around the room.

5 You could draw, colour and cut out two long ears and stick them onto a hair band, just like a hare's ears.

6 If you are going to make decorations for your room, the colours you should try to use are bright yellow and bright green, the type of colours you see outside in the gardens and parks.

Making Coloured Eggs

You will need

An egg for each person

A metal saucepan half filled with water

Vinegar

Food colouring

A small wax candle — a cake candle will do

Method

Put some food colouring into the saucepan and add one teaspoon of vinegar to every half a cup of water. Boil the eggs for ten minutes until they are hardboiled. Cool them off in some cold water and then take the candle and draw shapes on your egg.

Fill a bowl with water and add a different colour into the water. Remember to add the vinegar to the water. Place the eggs into the second colour and leave in the water for at least half an hour.

Lift the eggs up out of the water and your pattern will show on the egg in your first colour while the rest of the egg has been stained a different colour.

Some Little Prayers for the Spring Equinox

Ostara, you bring the spring, the hares, and the bird's eggs. Teach me to care a little more for all these creatures.

Thank you for the flowers that bloom in the spring, thank you for eggs and for chocolate!

Mother Goddess and Father God, bless all my family and my friends, and let them have eggs, chocolate or whatever it is that reminds them of springtime.

Beltane

Teachers, Parents and Guardians Notes

As many of you reading this will already know, Paganism is a fertility religion, those of us who follow this path celebrate the wonderful diversity of the flow of energy, the divine flow, you might call it "universal energy" that is within both male and female. This spark flows throughout the universe, throughout the world and flows into all of nature: plants, trees, animals, and human beings. Some say even rocks and water contain this spark of life. In all of nature, as it is in both the animal kingdom and in humans, this flows into two different main genders, male and female. We in turn think of our Deity as male and female, let's for this moment call these; Lord and Lady. The flow of spirit goes into both of these, male and female, but without these two joining, merging to become one, no creation can take place.

The earth may produce plants, but without the sun these will not grow. You may have a herd of mares but without a stallion you are never going to get any foals.

This moment when both the male and female energies blend into one is a very magical moment, a creative moment, and from this "magic" something new is seeded, this could be a thought, perhaps a story or a poem, it could be a painting, which will start in most cases with a drawing, or it can be a new being. It is this wonderful magical process that as Pagans we celebrate, the balance of both female and male that when they come together create something.

Now all of this is a very difficult idea for our young people to understand and to accept, it's not until we reach adulthood that we really begin to truly understand. And for some, this understanding comes much later in life, with the mundane world pushing many thoughts of Divinity, of Spirit, out of the way while we grow and learn.

So although we celebrate the Lord and Lady all year round, it is perhaps at Beltane when this comes to take centre stage and we may perhaps have someone in our group who takes the role of the Lord of the Forest, The Green Man or the Stag of the Forest, whichever name you wish to choose. We also have a Maiden/ Lover Goddess, the May Queen. She might be dressed in red, full of passion, ready and waiting to be joined to be married to the Lord of the Forest. These two people represent the male and female Divinity and in our celebration we need to join these two in order for the magical creation to take place.

In our group that we run in Glasgow in Scotland, we often choose a couple or if that's not possible we ask a May Queen to choose her "Green Man" who will stay as her partner for the day. We make a great fuss of our May Queen, putting a cloak around her, crowning her with a circlet of flowers and then we all take turns to tie little red ribbons onto the headdress, ribbons of prayer giving our intentions for a prosperous and creative year ahead. We often bind the wrists of the May Queen and the Green Man together, a symbolic way of joining; this is called "Handfasting" and in this case is done just for the day. (Although we have also been known to perform a Handfasting for a couple at Beltane for either a year and a day, a lifetime or eternity).

In the farmer's year, this is the point in time when the cattle, which have been in large sheds throughout the winter, will be let out and driven into the fields for the summer months. In days gone by, two large bonfires were lit and the cattle were driven between the two fires, this was both for purification and for fertility, and to this day bonfires are still lit on high hills to celebrate Beltane. There is a well-known "Beltane Fire Festival" in Edinburgh, which has its roots in these fires, which the farmers used.

Folk who followed the old ways will still burn some kind of fire, and if they have the chance it would be on the top of a hill. If not a bonfire, then a candle would be used to symbolise this magical fire.

A Note to the Grown-ups

It's very true that this festival is about the joining of the Goddess to the God, it's a fertility festival when in very ancient times a young women from the village may have been chosen to be joined to the God of Nature, The Stag of the Forest, and there would have been a young man chosen to represent him. We have no proof that this actually took place but many modern writers feel this would be the case. But there are many things that went on at this time of the year and for the sake of very young children, this story is about other aspects of Beltane.

A Story for Beltane

All the cows, the bullocks that were born last year and the bulls, were spending the winter in a huge barn on the farm where Iain lives with his family; he has an older brother and a little sister. His dad has a lot of fields, people said there were acres and acres, but a lot of them were up in the hills which had snow on them in the winter and the rain poured down the burns when it rained in the springtime.

It was time to turn all the animals out into the fields and because his family followed "the old ways" they had started to fetch wood, fallen branches, from all around the farm and build two big bonfires.

Iain's mum was busy cooking food for a feast they were going to have with their village friends and even his grandma and his aunties were busy getting ready for the celebration, soon it would be "Beltane".

The farmers would drive their beasts between the two bonfires and then up into the fields where they would graze all summer long. There were only two smaller cows that stayed close to the house, these provided fresh milk that they shared in the extended family.

Iain went out with his dad and other men who had come along to help and they rounded up all the cows, they drove them between the two bonfires and then up into the fields which had been covered in snow in the middle of the winter.

They were all tired when they came back, but this was not the end of the day because it was a special festival in the countryside.

At Beltane, there would be a holiday, the bonfires, lots of music and lovely things to eat. Many of the people who came to the celebration would wear clothes dyed red, or wear red ribbons in their hair. Iain would stay up until late listening to all the music and chatting with his friends. The day after was a holiday, no school, in fact, no one went to work, it was called "May Day".

In the towns and cities, some folk had forgotten about the time of year that the animals went out into the fields for the summer, but they did know it was time for a party and a day off.

At the Beltane celebration there was sometimes a "Handfasting" a kind of wedding when two people from the village were crowned, had their hands tied together and then kissed. After the May Day celebration, they would leave their parents' home and would go and live in their own house together. These were folk who had left school and college and had been going out to work and wanted to have more time together.

Iain and his family would talk to Herne, he was a God who people talked to at Beltane, the other name was the Stag, Lord of the Forest, and the Goddess was Belisana or if you prefer she was "The May Queen".

People who followed the old ways would ask the God and Goddess to bless their animals and their families; even the crops would be blessed. Sometimes they would ask a Druid to come and bless their animals and crops and, in some places, they would ask a priest.

Even in areas where all the people were now Christian, they still kept the May Day celebrations and would ask the local priest to come along and bless the animals, crops and even the people.

Things to Do at this Time of the Year

1 Make a circlet with ivy or twisted willow, then weave some red flowers into it, tie some red ribbons on it and choose someone to be "The May Queen".

2 Make a mask and stick leaves all over it, paint or draw them if you don't have any leaves. Put some thin elastic around the back and tie it onto the mask, then choose someone to be "The Green Man".

3 Tie the wrists of the May Queen and the Green Man loosely and ask them to stand in the middle of the room and then everyone should hold hands in a circle and dance around them. These two should have first choice of any snacks or cakes!

4 Cut strips of red and orange crêpe paper and attach them to your arms, run around the

room waving your arms and make big flames with the paper.

5   Ask the girls to wear wings and come as fairies and ask the boys to wear something green and come as green men.

6   Draw a big picture of a bonfire with lots of red and orange flames coming out of the fire!

7   Pretend to be bulls and cows and get "let out" of your winter barns and then run about making a noise like a bull or a cow.

8   Make some little cupcakes, then place them on a plate around in a circle and add some little icing sugar flowers.

Basic Cup Cakes

Makes 12

Ingredients
125g caster sugar
125g butter
4 tablespoons of either lemon juice or orange juice
The grated rind of two lemons or two small oranges
2 free range eggs
125g self-raising flour

For the icing
185g of sifted icing sugar
1 to 2 teaspoons of lemon juice or water.

Preparation and cooking times
Ready in 50 minutes

Method
Turn the oven on to 180C or 160C if it's fan assisted, gas mark 4.

1   Beat the sugar and butter together. If you have a grown-up helper, ask them to use an electric mixer for this part. Add in the grated rind and whisk until it is light and fluffy.

5   Beat the eggs in a little bowl and then add a little egg at a time into your mixture, keep mixing between times. If the mixture starts to curdle while you are adding the egg, sprinkle a little of the flour into your mixture.

3   Add in the flour by sprinkling it through a sieve into the bowl and fold the flour in with a metal spoon.

4   If the mixture starts to get too dry, add in the lemon or orange juice or use water, but do this carefully as too much will make the mixture too wet.

5   Take a big spoon of the mixture and hold it over the bowl, let it drop off the spoon and count one, two, three, your mixture should drop off your spoon at the count of three. Too soon and it's too wet, too slow and it's too dry.

6   Drop a teaspoon of the mixture into cup cake cases or small muffin cases and bake in a pre-heated oven for fifteen to twenty minutes, or until they have risen and look pale golden brown.

Take the cakes out of the oven when they are cooked and cool on a wire rack, your grown-up helper will do this part for you.

Once the cakes are cool, mix the icing sugar with a little water or lemon/orange juice and pour about half a teaspoon of icing onto each cupcake in turn.

You can decorate the cakes with different colours; use sweets, sprinkles, cherries, whichever matches your colour choice.

If you want to make different coloured icing, ask your grown-up helper to add some food colouring into your icing sugar mixture.

Little Prayers for Beltane

Light the bonfires, feel the heat, send the warmth to all I meet. Please help the plants to grow so we have a good harvest.

Thank you Mother Goddess for the love you share; help me to love just as you love me.

Blessings on you Lord of the Forest, may you run wild and free and bring us all many blessings.

Summer Solstice

Teachers Parents and Guardians Notes

Summer Solstice — The time when the days are at their longest and nights the shortest. It's dedicated to the Sun God and people would ask that the warmth and heat of the sun would ripen the grains. It's a very masculine festival and often in old times there would be games where the men would fight and the strongest male would be awarded a prize (known as the champion's portion). It's the first of three harvest festivals and this one is all about the corn grain.

Stonehenge is one of the world's best-known ancient sites and it springs into life with hundreds of New Age followers at the Summer Solstice. Folk gather round, talk, share stories, play drums, meditate and wait patiently for the sun to rise on the longest day and shine through a focal point in the stones. It was known that Druids would gather here but this only goes back a couple of hundred years; there seems to be a gap in records to link modern day Druidry to its ancient ancestors, and with good reason. And especially at midsummer many of us are not surprised to learn of a lack of records regarding the site's use at this time of year. But in recent years research has found that there are many burial sites within the stone circle and in the surrounding area. There is also a point at the Midwinter Solstice when the sun shines from the opposite direction and as it rises, shines into the circle and onto one of the inner stones, perhaps bringing new life, re-born life.

At Midsummer we reach a point in our circle of festivals when the male outweighs the female. The God, the Sun, is at his most powerful, it is his warmth, heat and light which brings the grain in the fields to maturity and we need all of this in order to feed the people.

There are in fact two points at this time of the year, the Summer Solstice on 21st June and a few days later, Midsummer Day, which is June 24th. And in the same way as folk would look at the length of days at midwinter to see if the sun had been reborn, here they looked to see if the sun was dying, losing strength or fading away.

Ancient Druids worshipped in oak groves, not in stone circles, they watched the movement of the sun and the stars and marked the turning of the year. Modern Pagans also tend to celebrate, rather than worship, out of doors, under the sky, in groves, fields, gardens and parks. But now as then we will call with thanks to Bel, the Sun God.

When Christianity came to these shores, the early Church re-dedicated the midsummer to St. John and all the ancient prayers which were said to Bel, were reworked for St. John the Baptist. It's curious that the well-known herb, St. John's wort widely used today has a major drawback, it can lead to an allergy to sunlight, something it shares with the likes of Pettitgrain and Bergamot.

A Story for the Summer Solstice

The Longest Day

There was a special grove in the next valley where Tansy lived with her parents and her extended family. It would take all day and part of the next day to get to it and they all went when the days were getting much longer. The whole village met each year with many other groups at this grove.

It looked a bit like a little wood but the trees were all oak and all stood strong and upright.

At the longest day, it was another special time, called the "Summer Solstice" and it happens every year when the sun stays shining in the sky for hours and hours, way past bedtime.

We don't have a very long sleep at this time, we feel tired before the sun goes to sleep and we want to carry on sleeping well after the moon goes to bed and the sun shines again.

And it was this time of year that Tansy and her family packed up their things, took blankets with them and food and went for a very long walk. They all followed a path right up the valley following the grown-ups.

They all became so tired that they camped overnight, sleeping under the stars, all cuddled up because when the sun did go to sleep it got cold, so Tansy cuddled up to her mum and stayed nice and warm.

The next day they walked over the hill and into the next valley where the oak grove was. They walked along the same path their ancestors had walked, all in a line. When they got there they found lots of people, some were selling things, some were cooking, and some were playing games.

As the sun went down everyone became quiet and stayed awake, sitting in groups or having a nap cuddled up together. Just before dawn, and just before the sun rose in the sky, everyone woke up and became very excited. They watched the sun rise and it shone into the circle of oak trees. The Druids blew down big trumpets and everyone cheered, the longest day had started.

Tansy and her family spent the day meeting people. Her dad bought a new cow and sold one of their young bulls. Some of the grown-ups had a chat and everyone made friends. Every family cooked food and many shared what they had with each other. Tansy and all the other children played lots of games until they were so tired they just fell asleep.

Things to Do at the Summer Solstice

1 Draw and paint a big sun, in yellows and pale orange, cut it out and put it up on the wall to remind you about the longest day.
2 Make several big trees by using tubes and cut-up cardboard boxes and paint them.
3 In the evening, draw the curtains and borrow a torch, then pretend the torch is the sun and make the sun climb up from underneath to shine on your tree circle, just as the sun does.
5 Try to wear something yellow or even gold, perhaps a yellow ribbon or a yellow t-shirt.
5 Eat yellow food for the day, sweetcorn, chicken, yellow fruit and custard. Or have a yellow snack, perhaps biscuits with cheese.
6 Make some little cakes and ice them with yellow icing, put yellow decorations on them.

Sunshine Yellow Sweetcorn Fritters

You will need

A bowl to mix the batter in
A metal spoon
A spatula to help with the mixing
A griddle or frying pan.

Ingredients

One small can of sweetcorn
One egg
Four tablespoons of maize floor or gram flour

One teaspoon of baking powder
Pinch of salt
Half to one cup of milk
Olive oil

Method* (needs a grown-up's help to cook)

Put the dry ingredients into the bowl and gently fold over with a metal spoon, make a well, a small dip in the middle of the flour and add the egg and some of the milk, little by little. Mix the batter into a thick consistency and then add in the drained sweetcorn. Mix all the corn evenly into the batter.

Put a little olive oil into the frying pan and when it's hot, drop one tablespoon of the batter into the pan, you should be able to get about six fritters into one pan at a time.

Turn from time to time until they are golden brown and have risen to twice their size.

Take out of the pan and drain on a piece of kitchen paper, keep repeating this until you have cooked all the mixture. The fritters can be kept warm in the oven.

You can serve these on their own with just some ketchup, or you can have them with an egg, or little sausages or bacon. You can even have baked beans over the top of them.

Little Prayers for the Longest Day

As the sun beats down and warms the ground, let it also warm my heart and all those that I love.

May the strength of this longest day fill my heart with warmth, let me show those I meet this warmth.

I am happy when I see the sun shine because I know that my Mother Goddess and Father God are sending me this light. Thank you for the sunshine.

Lughnasadh

Teachers Parents and Guardians Notes

Lughnasadh or in some places, Lammas, is either 1st or 2nd of August.

Lughnasadh is a Pagan holiday, often called Lammas, celebrating the first harvest and the reaping of grain. There are in fact three harvest festivals, which many Pagans keep. It is a cross-quarter holiday halfway between the Summer Solstice (Litha) and the Autumnal Equinox (Mabon). In the northern hemisphere, Lughnasadh takes place around August 1st with the Sun near the midpoint of Leo in the tropical Zodiac, while in the southern hemisphere Lughnasadh is celebrated around February 1st with the Sun near the midpoint of Aquarius. On the Wheel of the Year, it is opposite Imbolc, which is celebrated on February 2nd in the northern hemisphere, and late July / early August in the southern hemisphere.

Lughnasadh or Lammas is a time of thanksgiving for the start of the harvest. There is a Saxon word for the festival Half-mass. It was a major harvest festival all over Europe and different Gods were celebrated in different parts of the world: Ceres, Demeter, Juno, Augusta, and Lugh. Hence the name and why I refer to it as "Lughnasadh".

Lugh is a Sun God, a Grain God, and in some parts, his death is celebrated to feed his people. "John Barleycorn's death was his sacrifice in order to feed his children" (this is a well-known folk song).

The Lughnasadh plant is barley and this is said to belong to the element of Earth. It's ruled by Venus, which is the Mother/Lover aspect of the Goddess. A corn dolly, made of barley straw was made and hung up in the home to bring health and wealth. The straw was collected from "gleaning" around the edges of a field after the farmer had harvested the crop. The grain was used to make little barley cakes and the straw was used to make the dolly.

In some branches of the Pagan faith there is a very beautiful but sad ritual, the priestess who loves her God with all her heart has to symbolically slaughter him in order for the harvest to be gathered. The priest who takes on this role has to fall as if dead at the hands of his priestess and is then laid out on the ground. Anyone who is present is given a handful of grain and has the opportunity of gently throwing the grain over the body of the priest who in this case is taking on the role of the Grain God. If it's done correctly it is very moving and brings to mind that the spark of life, which flows into all things that grow on this Earth has to be cut down to be fed to the people, or to other animals. But it's never the end because some of the seed is then sown back into the ground to spring into life yet again.

These days it's difficult to be able to collect exactly the right grain and straw, so whatever grows in your area and is ripened by the sun, you could use. It's always a good idea to tune into the area you live and work, perhaps this is one way of doing just that.

For the Children

The Lughnasadh festival is a special time in the summer when the corn in the farmers' fields is ready to be picked, it's called harvesting. The corn grows green at first and then the sun ripens the corn and it turns a pale yellow. All the seeds at the top of the plant become plump and the top of the plant opens out.

The farmer takes his harvester, a big machine with wheels, and he drives it up and down the field cutting the corn, taking all the ears of corn off the plant and he leaves the stalks behind.

The farmer goes back another day and collects all the stalks, which become straw for the animal beds.

All around the outside of the field there are still a few plants of corn muddled up with grass and the animals eat this.

A Story for Lughnasadh

Lucy's dad grew his own corn, some of it was fed to the chickens, some fed to the cows and if he had any extra, he sold it to the other farmers or swapped it for something he needed.

This first harvest of the year was celebrated as a festival and the God that Lucy and her family talked to at this time was "Lugh", he was a Sun God and it was the heat of the sun that ripened the corn.

It was hot at this time of the year. Because her parents were busy, Lucy went for a walk along by the side of some of the fields that her dad had already harvested. As she walked, Lucy could see a woman, she seemed to be dressed in strange clothes, she was wearing a long red dress, and as she moved a little tinkling sound could be heard from a string of tiny bells tied around one of her ankles. She was crying so Lucy rummaged in her pocket for a tissue and walked up to her.

"Please don't cry," said Lucy. "Did you fall down and hurt yourself?"

The lady looked up at Lucy and seemed a little surprised that she was talking to her and offering her a tissue. But she smiled at Lucy and took the tissue to dry her tears.

"That's very kind of you my dear," said the lady. "I didn't fall down, but I was very sad because someone I love has died, but now I see you and your beautiful smile, I can see there is much to be happy about."

The lady stopped crying and dried her tears. She handed back the tissue to Lucy and stood up. "I must go now, but I often walk down this way so we may meet again one day, goodbye for now."

With that, the lady walked away and as Lucy started to put the tissue into her pocket, it seemed much bigger than before. When Lucy looked up again, the lady had gone, she must have walked very fast and with no shoes on her feet Lucy could not hear her footsteps.

Lucy turned back home and went to meet her mum because they were going to pick some grain from the edge of the fields.

Her parents were both in the kitchen having a quick break and a cup of tea. When Lucy arrived back home, she told her parents about the lady she had met. She then put her hand into her pocket to get the tissue so she could flush it away, but instead of a tissue in her pocket, she found grain, barley grain. Her dad came to help her and together they scooped up all the grain. "You seem to have been given some very good grain here," said Dad. "It's not mine, the grains are bigger and a slightly different colour. If I were you I would save this to sew in your garden. You will get some beautiful grain next year with it."

With that, her dad went back into the fields and left them together.

Lucy and her mum went down to the field after her dad had finished harvesting the corn and picked handfuls of what was left from around the edge of the field. They took it home and made a corn dolly, they wove the corn under and over, round and round. There are lots of different things you can make with left over corn, rattles, dollies, stars and Lucy's mum was very good at this.

Lucy helped her mum make a beautiful loaf of bread. They sprinkled just a few of the grains on the bread and baked it in a very hot oven. Then they held a special ceremony. They hung the corn dollies up inside the house, invited some friends to tea. They lit a candle, blessed the bread, and said a big thank you to Lugh for helping to ripen the corn.

Things to Do for Lughnasadh

1   If it's possible, go for a walk with your parents or teachers and collect some corn from around the edge of a field after the farmer has harvested the grain. Bring it back and make it into shapes with a grown-up to help you.

2   Make a loaf of bread with your parents or teacher, and if you can't make one from flour then ask Mum or another grown-up to buy something called a part-baked loaf and ask them to cook it in the oven. Fresh bread and butter will remind you all about the fields of grain and the farmers who collect it.

3   Draw a big sun picture and paint it with yellow and orange, give it lots of spikes called "rays" coming out from the middle of the sun.

4   This time wear something pale yellow, like sunshine. Maybe a yellow ribbon, maybe a pale yellow t-shirt?

5   Take a paper plate and stick strips of paper all around it, then paint it yellow and fix it onto the wall or on the windows.

6   When you are playing out in the sunshine, lift your arms right up towards the sky and say "thank you" for the beautiful sunshine.

Easy White Bread

You will need a grown-up helper for this recipe. It can be mixed in the evening, left in a warm damp place overnight and then cooked in the morning.

Makes 1 loaf

Preparation and Cooking Times

Prep 20 minutes

Cook 25 – 30 minutes

Plus 2 hours proving

Ingredients

500g strong white flour, plus extra for dusting

2 teaspoons salt

7g sachet fast-action yeast

3 tablespoons of olive oil

300ml water

Method

Mix the flour, salt and yeast in a large bowl. Make a well in the centre, then add the oil and water, and mix well. If the dough seems a little stiff, add 1-2 tablespoons of water, mix well then tip onto a lightly floured work surface and knead. Once the dough is satin-smooth, place it in a lightly oiled bowl. Leave to rise for 1 hour until doubled in size or place in the fridge overnight.

Line a baking tray with baking parchment. Knock back the dough, and then gently mould the dough into a ball. Place it on the baking parchment to prove for a further hour until doubled in size.

Heat oven to 220C or if you have a fan oven 200C or gas mark 7. Dust the loaf with flour and cut a cross about 6cm long into the top of the loaf with a sharp knife. Bake for 25–30 minutes until golden brown and the loaf sounds hollow when tapped underneath. Cool on a wire rack

Little Prayers for Lughnasadh

Lugh, you are strong and look after all of us who call your name. Thank you for being with us Lugh.

Thank you for the harvest, for bread and cake, please let all those I love have enough bread to eat this Lughnasadh.

It is sad to think that the plants have to be cut to collect the grain, but we know that the little seeds will make new plants next year, thank you for the seeds.

Autumn Equinox

Teachers, Parents and Guardians Notes

Autumn Equinox — is the second of the three harvest festivals and this one is all about the apples and other fruit that is gathered from the trees.

"Johnny Appleseed" and songs like this are all connected to this time of the year.

The Sun in its journey through the Zodiac belt reaches the constellation of Libra on 23rd of September. The symbol or the sign for Libra is often drawn or painted as scales — balance scales. And the Autumn Equinox is a time of perfect balance, day and night are once again exactly the same length. There is harmony here on Earth, the kind of harmony which leaves us with a feeling of happiness. In the countryside the harvest for all the grains is finished, in some places it's been finished for some time and in orchards all over these islands farmers are busy getting in the apple and pear harvest.

The apples are ripe and again in some places the job of collecting all these apples has already been done. In the earlier part of the 20th century, before the machines took over, groups of city dwellers would travel down to Kent and stay in huts for a couple of weeks or more. All day they would pick the apples from the orchards and they were paid by the barrel. In the evenings, they would gather around a fire, tell stories, sing songs and generally relax. This was their "holiday", it was a working holiday but it took them out of the smog of the cities for a couple of weeks, into the fresh air and sunshine.

These days all this is done by machine with just a few workers looking after the machines and doing odd jobs the mechanical beings cannot do.

So as we stop once again and pause on the great Wheel of the Year, it's another harvest festival and this time it's naturally all about the apple harvest. It was said years and years ago that if a village could have a good stock of apples, and there was also a good cheese maker, then they would all survive the winter and it was often only the apples and cheese that were left to eat at the end of a long cold winter.

There is a Goddess favoured by the Romans called "Pomona" who was celebrated at this time of the year but here, where I live, we simply call to the Mother Goddess or to Mother Earth. We would perhaps also call to "Father Sky" for the balance, but much of the ceremony will be to asking the elements to attend, and the blessing and teaching about the balance and the apple.

The apple is a perfect magical fruit to teach about the five elements: Air, Fire, Water, Earth and Spirit. Take one apple, cut it across the middle and open it up, where you should find a pip in each point, while the core seen this way around looks very much like a star.

A Note to the Grown-ups

I have chosen to associate this time of year to Danu, the Mother of the Celtic Gods. The festival falls in the east in a Druidcraft circle which is also linked to autumn. Danu had other names, *Danu of the Flowing Waters* amongst them. It can also be linked to the middle age of the Mother, someone who is in their "autumn years".

A Story for the Autumn Equinox

Long ago, when our ancestors lived on the land, they would have perhaps had a Druid living in their village or who otherwise may have visited at special times of the year.

Once again the little children, Tansy and Niall, had noticed that the day was as long as the night.

They heard the grown-ups saying something about "balance". Daylight would last just as long as night-time, so the village would have another festival, a gathering of friends and family.

This festival was another harvest, and perhaps the men would gather hops and make a kind of beer. Sometimes there were lots of apples ready on the trees. The days were still very warm here in Britain, but the nights had started to get a little bit chilly.

Everyone in the village was looking forward to a visit from the Druid. He was a very wise man who had studied for years. He played a little harp that he carried around with him and he told stories. It was good for Tansy and her cousin Niall to sit around a warm fire in the evening, with their families, all cuddled up to Mum or Dad and listen to the beautiful music and the stories of the Gods.

Tansy and Niall were getting excited and were spending the days doing their best to help their mums and dads, they were learning what fruit they could pick and which ones would give them a tummy ache.

The Druid arrived a day before the festival, he had walked for three days and three nights to get to their village in time to lead the celebrations. His feet were sore and he was tired from all the walking, so he came and spent that evening with Tansy's family. The Druid ate his meal with them and sat down to rest his poor sore feet.

Tansy sat down with him and asked him, "Who is special at this time of the year?" The Druid thought for a moment and looked down at little Tansy. "Well this is a time of harvest, for fruit and for some late grains. The Mother has been very good to us," he said.

"But the Mother Goddess was always special," said Tansy.

"Yes she is but because she has produced such a lot of fruit, grains and a few berries as well, I think we will make her a special feast."

"What's her name?" asked Tansy.

"She is known by different names in different places, but for here we will speak of her as Danu," explained the Druid.

Now Danu was the Mother of the Celtic Gods, she was sometimes called, Danu of the Flowing Waters, and many rivers all over the world are named after her.

Because the Mother Danu brings us such a lot to eat at this time of the year, we need to say a big think you and we must share some of our fruit and berries with the animals as well.

So that night the children went into their beds, wrapped up in furs because the night was cold, and they slept deeply and well, ready for the big festival the next day.

The sun was already up when the children awoke, they quickly got themselves ready and had some breakfast of hot cooked oats and had some fresh milk on the top with just a little honey to sweeten it.

Out in the middle of the village the Druid and elders of the village had already begun to make a special table, they had woven some willow, and made a basket, which they were filling with fruits, apples and berries. The women had already baked some bread, twisting the dough around to look like a braid.

People brought things to sit on, furs and pieces of animal hide and gradually the area filled up with people. There were drums, some pipes, and some people had shakers. These were hollow things perhaps made from hide and filled with dried seeds that made a wonderful noise when you shook them.

One of the women, an elder priestess and the Druid stood up and called the meeting to order, they asked everyone to be quiet and call for the Mother Goddess to join them. Everyone stayed very quiet but no one saw a Goddess, instead a red fox, a vixen, came walking towards the people. She walked all around the outside of the gathering, then went and sat down to watch.

The noise started; drums, pipes, singing, clapping and all the time the red vixen just sat and listened and watched.

The Druid called for a blessing on the harvest of fruit, and everyone prayed and thanked the Mother for all she had given them. Then the Druid took a smaller basket of fruit, which had a little handle, filled it with apples and berries and walked very slowly towards the fox, she never moved.

He put the basket down in front of the fox, took a step back and bowed. The fox stood up, bent her head down and then picked up the basket in her mouth and walked off out of the village and into the woods.

Everyone was very pleased. The fruit was shared out to all the families, and more taken to the outskirts of the woods and left there for the fairy folk.

There was dancing that night, and music and everyone had a lovely party.

And guess what happened the next day? Tansy and Niall were playing in the field next to the village when a red fox with an empty basket came walking towards them, they stood very still and bowed like the Druid had done, and the fox bent her head, dropped the basket and then walked off again.

Tancy and Niall took the basket back to the Druid who was still staying in the village and he looked very surprised, and said, "Children, you have been noticed by the Mother and she is pleased with you for being such good children, learn your lessons well and work hard, you will work for the Goddess one day yourself."

Why do you think he said that? You don't know? Then I shall tell you.

Some folk say that the Goddess Danu is able to change herself into a red fox, a lady fox called a vixen. She walks around freely and not many know which one she is, so next time you see a red fox, stand still and whisper to her, "Bless you Mother" and if it's her she will look you straight in the eye and bless you with her thoughts.

Things to Do for the Autumn Equinox

1   Paint some pictures of green grass, countryside and nature, and put them on a table.
2   Bring some apples and other fruit and put them in a basket on your table, in the middle of your pictures.
3   Make a shaker with an empty crisps tube, ask your parents or your guardian to give you some dried lentils or peas or seeds and put them in the tube. Block the end off or just put the lid back on and when you shake it, you have a wonderful sound.
4   You can make a longer tube and use small seeds, block the ends off and gently tip in from side to side, it will sound like water running over pebbles.
5   Ask your teacher or whoever is looking after you for an apple, ask them to cut it right across the middle, not from the stalk to the bottom, around its middle. Look inside and you will see a magic star made from seeds. (Because apples are special fruit, everyone should eat apples!)
6   If you have more time, you can make apples or berries from moulding dough or clay, let them dry and paint them green and red.
7   You can have an autumn party, make some music and sing some songs all about this time of year.

Fruit Salad with Apples and Pears

You will need

Apples
Pears
Berries

A small sharp knife that your grown-up helper will need to use

A lemon

Lemon squeezer

A little fruit juice

A bowl to put all the fruit in

Method

Ask your grown-up helper to peel and cut the apples and pears while you take all the stems and leaves off the berries. Wash your berries under a cold-water tap.

Cut the apples and pears into small pieces, put them in the bowl and squeeze some of the lemon juice over them. You may need to add a little apple juice or water at this point to cover the apples and pears. If the berries are large, then cut them in half. Mix all the fruit together in the bowl and if necessary add a little more lemon juice.

Put the fruit salad into the fridge to cool down, taste to see if it needs any sugar and if it does, sprinkle a little sugar over the salad and mix.

You can eat this fruit salad as a snack, or as a pudding with some ice cream or fresh cream. If you don't eat dairy products, then use some soya cream in its place.

Some Little Prayers for the Autumn Equinox

Danu of the Flowing Waters, wash me nice and clean and let me sing and dance with happiness.

Goddess you are wise, I am very small but with your help I'm going to grow bigger and better.

Father Sky, walk with me until I grow wise, and then teach me to help others become wise too.

Samhain

Teachers, Parents and Guardians Notes

Samhain — (sow-een) is the Celtic New Year, the festival to remember our dead; we refer to them as ancestors and ask them to join with us in our celebrations. It is also the third harvest festival, which is the Berry Harvest.

It's difficult to talk about Samhain these days without going into Halloween, which took its name from "All Hallows Eve". It was the night before All Saints Day in the established Church calendar. This is another situation where the people already had a festival to honour their dead and nothing would stop them. So the festival was at one point given a Christian blessing and everyone still remembered their dead and still went to their grave-yards and cleaned up the family grave, and perhaps left a light burning by the headstone.

This seems to date back to pre-Christian times when it was said that the unseen veil between this world and the next is very thin at this time of year and that spirits are often seen, heard and felt. For Pagans this is a special time of year when we do indeed remember our loved ones who have moved on from this life to the next. Many of us speak of this place as "the Summerlands" a place where it's always summer, there is no pain, no suffering and it is said that our loved ones will rest in the care of our ancestors until their spirit has recovered from their life here on earth and perhaps their death.

Because this time of year has been taken over by the American "trick or treating" and countless costumes are available in the shops, it's perhaps difficult for a Pagan family to know just which way to handle this. I suggest to our group that when we meet for this festival that they do indeed come in costume. Most of them choose to come as witches, walking through the park and then into the café afterwards in their costumes and no one minds at all. It is the one time of the year that if you wish to dress in your robes, or as an ancient Pagan, a wizard or a Druid, it all adds to the atmosphere. However, we don't suggest our people go collecting sweeties from the strangers we meet on our walk through the park.

The children dress up for a party at school, they decorate their classrooms with spider's webs, orange pumpkins, skeletons and flying witches, who would want to spoil their fun, but teachers please note, there is a serious side to this time of year and that is to remember with respect our ancestors of line, blood and place.

Here in Glasgow it is also the time of the year when we wake the Winter Goddess, Bheara called the "Cailleach" meaning "sharp" or "veiled one". Not everyone in the Pagan world wakes the Winter Goddess, but we do make a point of this festival as being the end of summer and the start of winter, and some say that Brigit will then go into the under-world and give her place to Bheara or to the winter. The Winter Goddess will walk the hills and valleys, she will shake her white shawl and her feather bed, and this will fall as snow.

A Story for Samhain

At the school the teachers were starting to get ready for Halloween, they talked together over coffee about the decorations they would have, orange pumpkins and spiders' webs, ghosts and other scary things. They were going to have a party, a day when the children could come in a costume or bring a costume to change into. Later they told the children what they were planning.

Lucy went home to talk to her mum about it, she was not pleased because little Lucy followed the old ways, as did her mum, she was a Pagan. She loved the Mother Goddess and the Father God, she loved nature and she especially loved animals.

You see, for Lucy and children like her this time of year was called "Samhain" (pronounced "Sow-een") and it was the time of year when they remembered their ancestors, the people who had lived here before. Lucy and her family, her friends and her mum's friends remembered those they loved who had died and gone to the Summerlands.

What's the Summerlands? It's a place where the spirit of the person, the spark inside them that brings them to life, goes after they die. This is where it's always summer, where the grass is always green, where flowers and butterflies are all year round. A beautiful place where there is no pain, no war, and no fighting.

We think that our loved ones go there and have a nice rest, and their spirit grows strong again, they have a drink from "the well of forgetfulness" and all the nasty things that may have happened in their life are forgotten.

So Lucy was not happy, she thought her school did not understand that they should remember their loved ones that had gone to the Summerlands and also those people who had lived here long before her.

Lucy did not want to be a ghost, or a pumpkin, or a spider, she wanted to wear her witch's hat, and a cloak and carry her cauldron. (That was a black pot with a handle that she burnt incense in, with her mum's help.)

Lucy and her Mum went to school the next day to talk to the teacher, and to try to explain that she and her family were Pagan and thought this time of year was a special time to respect their dead, their ancestors.

Miss Teacher knew very little about such things, she did not have any spiritual path and she was very surprised to find out how upset Lucy had been. She was a very nice person and never wanted to make any of her children unhappy, so she sat and listened to all that Lucy's mum had to say.

When the chat was over, Miss Teacher made her mind up to make sure all the children knew the story behind all of the fuss people made about Halloween.

Several hundred years ago, many people who lived in the countryside still marked the years turning with different festivals through the year and when it came to the Full Moon at the end of October or early November they gathered together, under the moonlight to remember their ancestors and especially those loved ones who had died and gone to the Summerlands. It was very dangerous to travel around at night so they dressed themselves up in costumes. If they met anyone they pretended to be a ghost and frightened folk into thinking they had seen a ghost. So "guise" or disguise became normal at this time of the year.

After many years, the Church of the land could not stamp out all of this, as the people still carried on the practice. They therefore made a special day in their year, "All Saint's Day", and the next day they called "All Soul's Day" and asked the people to go and pray for all the souls and saints. The people did more than that, they took a bucket of water and a scrubbing brush, went and cleaned their family grave and left a candle in a holder on the grave overnight.

Why would you think they would do this? Well, to keep away the ghosts who they thought they would meet if they went out at night.

Who were they really seeing? They were seeing people who followed the Pagan year and who dressed up in disguise so no one knew who they really were.

There is one more thing you should know … they say that the veil between this world and the next world is very thin at this time of the year and fairy folk, spirits of people who had once lived here, can sometimes be seen!

What should you do?

When I was three years old, my nanny taught me that if ever I see a ghost I should say to them, "Go in peace" and they will. So never be afraid of the dark or of things that go bump in the night, just follow this advice and all will be well.

So what happened in Lucy's school that year? Well, the class made a special memory table and asked the children to bring photos of any of their family that were no longer with us, the ones that had already gone to the Summerlands. And they put some flowers in a vase on the table and wrote on a card "we remember with love".

And they still had a party, they all dressed up in costumes, and they played silly games, but the children all knew that this time was a special time for those people who were Pagan.

I heard that some of the children in the class made their parents bring a bucket of water and a scrubbing brush and clean up great-granddad's grave, they even left a little candle next to the gravestone overnight on October 31st.

So when you get ready to go "trick or treating" and gather up lots of sweets, apples and nuts from the doors of those who have decorated their homes, just remember that this is the time of year to remember.

If we never had ancestors, we would not be here today, for they are the folk who walked this earth before us, who lived and died and made this the place it is now.

Things to Do for Samhain

Cover a little table or part of a table with a cloth or make some pictures of green grass with butterflies, then put photos of anyone from your family who has gone to the Summerlands on the table. This will be your memory table.

Carve out a pumpkin with the help of your teachers or your parents/guardians and make holes in the shell to let the light out. Then ask a grown-up to put a little candle, a tea light, into the middle of the empty pumpkin and when it's dark, light the candle and the light will shine through the holes and make a lantern.

Paint a picture of a spider's web, then with a black cotton wool ball and some pipe cleaners, make a spider and stick it in the middle of the web. Put the picture up on the wall.

Make a witch's hat by using a large paper plate, paint it black, cut a piece the shape of a slice of cake out of it and bring the edges together to make a cone. Take another plate and cut out the centre of it and stick the cone onto the edges of the second place. You will need a grown-up to help you with this. You can use this witch's hat to add to your decorations or if it's big enough you can put some elastic into the brim and wear it!

Go out where there are nut trees or bushes, with either your teacher or your parents or guardians, find some nuts, hazel nuts or beach nuts and perhaps some late berries, and bring them back to decorate your memory table. Or you can have a nature table as well.

Leaves this time of year are turning all shades of brown, rust and gold, and you can collect some of these and stick them onto paper to make a leaf pattern. Find out what leaves they are and which kind of tree they came from.

*Parents, Teachers and Guardians, you can find instructions on how to carve a pumpkin here: http://www.pumpkincarving101.com/ you will need a pumpkin carving knife, some old newspaper to cover your table and perhaps a bowl for all the fruit, which you may want to cook with.

Samhain Cakes

Using the basic cup cake recipe, make some orange butter icing and decorate with chocolate spiders and little pumpkin decorations.

Orange Butter Icing

75g soft butter
140g icing sugar, sifted
Orange food colour

Method

To make the icing, beat the soft butter and add the colour and the icing sugar little at a time. Beat it until it is very soft and every bit of the icing sugar has been mixed in.

Scoop a teaspoon of the butter icing onto the top of your cup cake, use a fork to make little peaks in the icing and then decorate with a chocolate spider or a pumpkin or other seasonal decoration.

Some Little Prayers for This Time of Year

At this time of year, we remember our ancestors, our loved ones who have left us to go to the Summerlands. We know you are only a thought away and we send you our love and we ask that you send us your love back.

Winter Goddess, we ask you to wake up now, it's time for you to walk around the hills and valleys and shake your feather bed, letting it fall as snow on the hills. Welcome Winter Goddess. (Her name amongst Celtic people is Cailleach)

Sister Moon, as the nights grow very cold and frosty, shine your light over the hills, valleys and through the streets, so those people who are travelling around will be able to see. Thank you Sister Moon!

Mother Goddess, Father God, we know you are looking after us and helping the seasons change. We want to thank you for all that you do for us. Please continue to watch over our families both those in this world and those in the Summerlands.

Midwinter and Yuletide

Teachers, Parents and Guardians Notes

The Wheel of the Year turns around again and we reach the point for the Midwinter Solstice, the longest night of the year. This is the point at which the Sun is furthest away from where we are here on Earth. (We actually know it is the Earth that is moving and not the Sun but did our ancestors?) I am in Scotland and this happens on 21st or 22nd December but you may perhaps be elsewhere in the world and your Mid-winter could well be June 21st or 22nd. To our ancestors it looked for all the world as if the sun was dying, or going away, perhaps never to come back. So our ancient Wiseman, Druid, Shaman, those who kept a careful note of sunrise and sunset, would watch very carefully. About four days later, he would report back to the rest of the village that the sun was coming back, had been re-born and at that point they would most certainly have a party!

From one point of view, a Pagan point of view, we might explain it in this way: The Mother Goddess will labour all night long to give birth to the new Sun, the Solar Deity, the tiny God. We will light candles for her, sing to her, pray that she will be successful and that the Divine God, the power that inspires us, brings us warmth and strength would come back to us. If you look very carefully, it is about three days and three nights before you notice the length of the day increasing. You can begin to see a well-known pattern, the number three!

There are many animals connected to this time of year. We have the well-known reindeer who pull the sleigh around the world in order for Santa to bring gifts to children on the 25th December. We have "Mother Goose" or Frau Holle, the winter Goddess who shakes her feather bed all over Europe bringing the snow, and in northern Europe we have the Yule Goat, most likely descended from the Norse God Thor, who rode through the sky on a chariot drawn by two Goats. In Scandinavia and in Northern Europe the 'Yule Goat' is a well-known decoration these days made of straw tied with red ribbons.

We hold a Midwinter Solstice ceremony each year, for us it is normally early to allow the members to have more time with their families over the festive period. But if you are on the other side of the world, then you no doubt will be able to hold your ceremony on the day itself, or very close to it.

The party, the celebration, which our country dwelling ancestors would hold once they were told that the sun had been re-born was called "Yule". A large log, almost a tree trunk would be brought into the main hall or gathering place and lit in the middle, a feast would take place and the people would rest, eat and drink, and entertain each other with songs and stories. Each day the two ends of the log would be pushed into the middle of the fire and the party would continue for what is now known as the twelve days of Yuletide.

This is another Pagan festival that has been taken over by the early Christian Church and is now almost secular. Research tells us that the "Star of Bethlehem" was in fact a conjunction of two major planets in the sky. In 1614, the German astronomer Johannes Kepler determined that a series of three conjunctions of the planets Jupiter and Saturn occurred in the year seven BCE. There would be one conjunction as the planets lined up as seen from Earth with the naked eye, and then because of the orbit of the Earth, they would appear to come apart again, or travel backwards. There would then be a second conjunction when the planets lined up and yet a last third before they drew apart. This took place on 15th September and ran into early October on the years around seven BCE (possibly five BCE).

So Jesus, if indeed he was born, would have been born around September or October and not at the Midwinter. But the people had celebrated the birth of their Divine Child, the child of inspiration, warmth and heat three days and nights after the Midwinter Solstice, so the festival was re-named "Christ-Mass" and everyone kept the dates of Midwinter and Yuletide which became "Christmas".

It appears that this Christian God has two birthdays, a real one and a symbolic one as well. Just like our Queen who also has two birthdays an official one and a real one, marking the moment when she took her first independent breath.

We don't stop our children celebrating Christmas, they all have presents, they all look towards "Santa" coming in the night and bringing them new toys. We tend to speak of it as 'Yuletide' amongst ourselves. The reason is that Pagan parents do not believe in pushing their own personal beliefs onto our children. We believe that they should learn about all religions and once they get to an age when they can choose for themselves which spiritual path is right for them, we will then do what we can to support them. If they want to come along and join in with us, then we do not stop them, but neither do Pagan parents that I know of stop their teenagers going along to church, or stop them learning about any other religion. Each person is an individual and needs to make their own mind up as to which path is right for them. We would just seek to teach them and show them what our own ancestors may have done.

A Story for Midwinter

Tansy was three years and six moons old. She had her third Solar return last summer when the old Druid told her that the Sun had once again come round to the same place as it had been the day she was born. Tansy spent a lot of time visiting the Druid because she did not have to do any chores yet because she was too small to carry water, too small to cook over the fire and too small to shake the fur skins that her family slept under at night.

The days had been getting shorter and shorter and the nights seemed to be getting longer and longer, Tansy didn't understand why all this was happening so she went to visit the Druid again and asked him.

"Well," replied the Druid. "It happens every year like this and soon we will have to wait to see if the Sun will be re-born and start to grow stronger again."

"Tell me what we have to do," asked Tansy.

So the Druid sat down and told her all about the longest night and the days to wait afterwards. "As the Sun grows weaker and weaker and further away from our land we are taken over by longer and longer nights. Soon now the night will become so long that we must light a fire to welcome the return of the light. Far away in a distant land where Gods and Goddess live the Mother of the Gods is carrying the new Sun, on the longest night she will spend all night bringing the new light into the World, a Sun re-born at Midwinter to bring warmth and light to us all. So we will all meet, in the darkness and we will light one fire, from there all other fires will be lit and we will welcome the new Sun, the Divine Child of Midwinter back into our world."

"Then what?" asked Tansy.

"Ahh, that's only the start," said the Druid. "We must measure the light each day to see if it is growing, if it is we shall celebrate and have a feast."

And so Tansy and her family, with all the people from the village met on that longest night and from the darkness lit one single fire, then all the homes in the village took a piece of the fire to start a new light.

Each day the Druid measured the length of the daylight until on the fourth day he announced that the Sun was growing in strength and we had a slightly longer day!

At that point, Tansy's father brought a big log of oak into the main village hut and it was lit in the middle, they had a big feast with lots to eat and lots to drink.

This, the Druid told Tansy was called "Yule" and happened every year after Midwinter.

Things to Do for Midwinter and Yule

1 Draw a picture of a standing stone with a little bit of yellow light touching its top. You can decorate the stone with glitter.

2 At this time of year you can make some Yule cards, try drawing holly leaves on your card and stick some red little cotton balls for berries.

3 Paint a picture of the Yule log with nice red flames in the middle.

4 With your grown-ups make some paper chains and decorate the room.

5 Make some biscuits with your grown-ups, cut them out in shapes of holly leaves, and the shape of that cheerful chap dressed in red who comes to visit bringing presents … what's his name?

Holly and Santa Biscuits

Use the basic biscuit recipe and method earlier in the book, in the section about Imbolc. Instead of using a moon cutter, use a holly leaf cutter or a Santa cutter, or you can even use a fir tree shaped cutter.

Once your biscuits are cooked, make a little bit of icing sugar and then add some coloured balls onto the biscuits. You can make trees that look as if they have decorations on them or use small red balls at one end of the holly leaf for the berry.

Some Little Prayers for Midwinter and Yule

As the nights grow longer and longer, give me patience to wait for the newborn light.

Remind me Mother Goddess that I am your child and help me be kind to both people and to animals.

Bless me, my family and friends, this long night and teach us all to be happy and welcome the new light

Let's Talk About the Moon

A Prayer for Teachers, Parents and Guardians

Mother we know you have been called by different names, in different times and by different peoples.

We know you are Maiden, Mother and Wise Women.

As the seed grows in the ground, help me to teach the children in my care about the beauty of your world, of its lands and seas, forests and rivers.

Like a maiden, help me to skip with the young, to see with young eyes.

Like a mother, always give me the time to love these children.

In your wisdom, give me patience and understanding in my dealing with these children.

Father, you are born at Midwinter and grow strong and warm the earth, and you answer to different names for different peoples.

We know you as youth, as lover and as wise man and elder.

Help me to stand up to the battles each day brings, give me strength yet kindness in my dealings with the children in my care.

Then as day turns to night, give me energy and love to share with my partner.

As the year turns, so my years will turn also, give me the wisdom to try to understand these children in my care.

Father, as you stand side by side with the Goddess, help me to stand side by side with my partner and those I work with, give me your strength to protect these children in my care.

As above, so below.

Blessed be!

For the Children

Now we all know that the Moon is a rock that orbits the Earth and that the light, which shines from the Moon is a reflection from the Sun. It's quite nice to imagine the Moon as having a life, which only lasts one month.

A Story About the Moon

Everything was dark in the night sky, thousands of stars and planets all across the universe were twinkling, but the Moon was nowhere to be seen.

The Sun God, let's give him a simple name shall we ... "Solar", he looked everywhere for the Moon, who we shall call "Lunar" and could not find her so he took a deep breath and blew out some bright golden light and far below in the dark a tiny particle of this touched the sleeping Lunar.

She stretched and yawned, and tried to stand up, but she was still a baby and couldn't stand, so she lay down and waited for some more particles from Solar to reach her. The next night she tried again and managed to stand up and stretch. A tiny silver light ran all up and down her and she stretched up towards the night sky and leaned over to bow very slightly to Solar.

Night by night she grew and by the third night she had enough silver light to shine a thin crescent back to the people on the earth. The people were so happy, they welcomed her back and left little bowls of milk out all night so she could drink and grow.

Lunar was soon running around, she came down and ran around the forests and she ran around the valleys and through the towns and cities. She danced and played with the cats, and the wolf, and she sat on the edge of the lake and shone little ripples of light across the top of the water. The fish popped up to say "Hello Lunar, welcome back".

As she grew bigger and stronger, Solar saw how very beautiful she was and smiled to her. "Soon," he said. "You will dance with me all day and all night." And the two fell in love.

As the nights went by Lunar realised she was getting bigger and her tummy was getting rounder and rounder. She was so full of beautiful magical silver light and all she could do was to sit in the night sky. She gave all her magic to all the mothers on the Earth. She sent her silver light to watch over their labours as they too gave birth to their babies. She shone on all the plants and flowers, and many of them that bloomed at night opened their petals and lots of moths came out to drink their nectar.

The people on the earth met up together as Lunar grew huge and round and full in the night sky, they used her magical rays to put into different things they made to make people better. They met up in little groups all over the place and sang songs to Lunar.

One night she was completely full and round, Solar was so happy he blew on her and for some she looked almost golden with his love.

As the nights went on Lunar became a little tired so she let her long dark hair fall across part of her face, so nobody could see how tired she was. But the people knew and understood and called to her, "You are gaining your wisdom Lunar, we welcome your time of wisdom teach us to be wise also."

So Lunar came down and walked around the earth, she visited many different groups, she talked with the older mothers and then on later nights she spoke to the grandmothers and the elders in society. She taught them all the wisdom she knew.

One night, not long before the end of her life, Lunar spoke to the elders and said, "Soon I will be gone and you are to have a big clean up, do not do any magic, instead clean your homes and your work places for I will return but as a tiny baby."

The grandmothers and grandfathers spoke to the younger people and told them that soon Lunar would no longer be with them. In the sky, Solar was sad, but he knew what would happen and although he loved Lunar, he also knew her life must come to an end.

Then one night it was so very dark, Solar was sad and sorry to have lost his Lunar. The people on earth took a bucket and cloths and they cleaned their homes, they cleaned their work places and they trimmed their hair and got themselves all cleaned up and ready for the tiny baby.

And on the next night, Solar saw a tiny little flicker and he knew that a little Lunar was growing deep in the night sky, he blew hard to spread his particles and the tiny little Lunar wriggled happily and slept.

Each month now, Solar and Lunar go through the same thing, she is born, he blows energy and particles to her and she grows and grows. She falls in love with Solar and each month he falls in love again and Lunar grows huge and big.

And so it has always been and always will be for millions of years to come!

So in each month there is a New Moon, a Full Moon and a Wise Moon.

The New Moon links with all things small, new and has lots of bright energy, and at the Full Moon her magic is very strong and she links with mothers and has lots of magic. At the end of the month, we have a Wise Moon who has seen all things and gives advice, tells the gardeners when to cut branches, cut the grass and clear away old unwanted growth. She links with older people, wise people.

And in the dark of the Moon when we have no moonlight it's not a good idea to go out at night, instead it's a very good time to have a cleanup, a tidy up ready for the New Moon again.

Things to Do for a Dark Moon (that is the nights when it's completely dark with no moon at all):

1   Tidy up your toys, books and empty your rubbish bin. Make sure all your dolls are tidy, perhaps if you have a toy farm, put all your animals back into their pens, if you have a train set, shunt them into their sheds or put them at the end of the line. And if you have some soft toys, sit them all up in a tidy line.

2   If you have been painting or chalking, now is the time to make sure your brushes are clean and ready to paint a new picture.

3   Ask if you can have a bath before bedtime or a shower and wash your hair because very soon, in a night or two there will be a tiny bright new moon!

Things to Do for a New Moon

1 Make a start at a new project, perhaps a new painting or drawing.
2 If you do have any seeds and it's the springtime, now is the time to plant your seeds and water them carefully. The strength of the moon growing day by day will encourage your seeds to grow.
3 Ask a grown-up to take you out when it's dark to look in the sky for the New Moon, see if you can find the tiny sliver of light in the sky. (Your grown-up help will have to check to see when the moon gets up where you live).

Things to Do for a Full Moon

1 It's a nice time for a small party, you could drink milk, have white bread and butter, cake with white icing. Or if you don't like milk, how about lemonade?
2 You could paint a Full Moon picture, with the dark blue sky and lots of stars, or if you don't want to paint it, then perhaps use crayons or coloured pencils.
3 If you have any new semi-precious gemstones, you could put them on the windowsill to bathe in the moonlight. Ask a grown-up to help you with this.

Things to Do for a Wise Moon

1 If you don't want your hair to grow too quickly, then ask a grown-up to cut your hair at this time. (If you want it to grow very quickly, have it cut at the Full Moon).
2 Go through your toys, if you have any that are broken, perhaps it's time to either throw them away or ask a grown-up to mend them for you.
3 Have a tea and this time try some brown bread and butter, and have cakes with dark coloured icing. Drink darker drinks, tea, or perhaps dark juice like blackcurrant.

Some Prayers for the Times of the Moon

Beautiful silvery Moon, shine on me tonight, let your light brighten each night giving us sound, peaceful sleep.

Diana, Goddess of the Night, of the Moon, brighten my mind and let me use your energy for good things.

Diana, shine your silver light deep down to my toes, help me feel what others feel and learn to understand about feelings.

Source Materials

Natural Magic, A Seasonal Guide, by Paddy Slade.

Practical Paganism, by Antony Kemp & J.M. Sertori.

A Witches Bible, the Complete Witches Handbook, by Janet and Stewart Farrar.

Progressive Witchcraft, by Janet Farrar and Gavin Bone.

A Ceremony for Every Occasion, Through the Pagan Wheel of the Year and Rites of Passage, by Siusaidh Ceanadach

The Pagan Religions of the Ancient British Isles, by Ronald Hutton

Fifty Years of Wicca, by Frederic Lamond

Moon Books invites you to begin or deepen your encounter with
Paganism, in all its rich, creative, flourishing forms.

Printed and bound by CPI Group (UK) Ltd, Croydon, CR0 4YY